A NOTE TO PARENTS

When your children are ready to "step into reading," giving them the right books—and lots of them—is as crucial as giving them the right food to eat. **Step into Reading Books** present exciting stories and information reinforced with lively, colorful illustrations that make learning to read fun, satisfying, and worthwhile. They are priced so that acquiring an entire library of them is affordable. And they are beginning readers with an important difference—they're written on four levels.

   Step 1 Books, with their very large type and extremely simple vocabulary, have been created for the very youngest readers. **Step 2 Books** are both longer and slightly more difficult. **Step 3 Books,** written to mid-second-grade reading levels, are for the child who has acquired even greater reading skills. **Step 4 Books** offer exciting nonfiction for the increasingly proficient reader.

   Children develop at different ages. **Step into Reading Books,** with their four levels of reading, are designed to help children become good—and interested—readers *faster*. The grade levels assigned to the four steps—preschool through grade 1 for Step 1, grades 1 through 3 for Step 2, grades 2 and 3 for Step 3, and grades 2 through 4 for Step 4—are intended only as guides. Some children move through all four steps very rapidly; others climb the steps over a period of several years. These books will help your child "step into reading" in style!

Text copyright © 1989 by Random House, Inc. Illustrations copyright © 1989 by S. D. Schindler. All rights reserved under International and Pan-American Copyright Conventions. Published in the United States by Random House, Inc., New York, and simultaneously in Canada by Random House of Canada Limited, Toronto.

Library of Congress Cataloging-in-Publication Data:
Hautzig, Deborah. The Pied Piper of Hamelin / by Deborah Hautzig ; illustrated by S. D. Schindler. p. cm.–(Step into reading. A Step 2 book) SUMMARY: Rats are everywhere in the town of Hamelin, until the Pied Piper plays his magic flute. ISBN: 0-394-86579-0 (pbk.); 0-394-96579-5 (lib. bdg.) 1. Pied Piper of Hamelin (Legendary character). I. Schindler, S. D., ill. II. Pied Piper of Hamelin. English. III. Title. IV. Series: Step into reading. Step 2 book. [DNLM: 1. Pied Piper of Hamelin (Legendary character) 2. Folklore–Germany (West)–Hamelin] PZ8.1.H3Pi 1989 398.21'0943 [E]–dc20 89-3968

Manufactured in the United States of America   7 8 9 0

STEP INTO READING is a trademark of Random House, Inc.

Step into Reading

THE PIED PIPER OF HAMELIN

By Deborah Hautzig

Illustrated by S. D. Schindler

A Step 2 Book

Random House New York

Hamelin was a lovely town.

It had pretty little houses

and cobblestone streets.

And it was next to

a great, wide river.

But Hamelin had a problem.

Hamelin had rats.

Everywhere you looked,

there they were.

They chased the dogs.

They killed the cats.

They even bit little babies

in cradles.

The rats made nests in shoes

and boots and hats.

When the poor tired people

went to bed, rats were waiting for them.

They nibbled the people's toes

so they could not sleep.

The rats liked kitchens
best of all.
They ripped open sacks of food
with their sharp little teeth.
They ate the flour and sugar.
They ate the corn and rice.

10

They even jumped onto the table
when families sat down to eat.
The rats ate and ate.
And the people of Hamelin
began to starve.

At last the people

went to the Town Hall.

"We want to see the Mayor!"

they shouted.

The doorkeeper peeped out.

"The Mayor is busy!" he told them.

But the people would not leave.

"We will not go away

until we see him!" they cried.

Finally the Mayor came out.

The Mayor was a fat, proud man.

He always wore jewels

and robes of fur.

But today he looked small and scared.

"My people, we are doing

all we can about this problem..."

he said.

"But nothing has worked!"

cried the people.

"Think! Use your brains!

Rid us of these rats—

or WE will get rid of YOU!"

The Mayor sat down with his council.

He tried to think of what to do.

"We could put out poison," he said.

"We tried that already,"
  said his council.

"The rats were too clever!

  They left the poison and ate our food!"

"Can we lay traps?"

asked the Mayor.

The councilmen shook their heads no.

"There are too many rats.

We could never lay enough traps!"

The Mayor and his council

talked all day and all night

about Hamelin's terrible problem.

At dawn there was a tap at the door.

In came the strangest man!

He was tall and thin.

He had sharp blue eyes.

He wore a long coat

that was yellow, red, and blue.

And around his neck

hung a pipe.

"Who are you?" asked the Mayor.

The strange man said this:

"People call me the Pied Piper

because of my colorful coat.

I hear you have troubles.

Well, your troubles are over."

"What do you mean?"

asked the Mayor.

"I have a secret charm,"

said the Piper.

"It will make any creature follow me.

If you pay me a thousand guilders,

I will rid this town of rats—

every single one!"

The Mayor's mouth fell open.

"That's impossible!" he cried.

"I will show you," said the Piper.

"Will you pay me

a thousand guilders?"

"If you get rid of the rats,"

said the Mayor,

"I'll pay you FIFTY thousand!"

"Done," said the Piper with a smile.

The Piper went into the street.

He lifted his pipe to his lips

and began to play.

After only three notes,

rats came running into the street.

Big rats, small rats,

fat rats, thin rats,

thousands of rats—

they gathered around the Piper

and followed him.

The Piper walked through Hamelin

playing his tune.

People dropped their work

and ran to watch him.

"Look!" cried a little lame boy.

"He is going to the river!"

When the Piper came to the river,

he stopped.

But the rats did not.

They kept on running

as if they were under a spell.

They ran right into the river

while the Piper played.

And when his tune was over,

all the rats had drowned.

The people of Hamelin

went wild with joy!

They rang the bells

and sang and danced.

No one sang louder than the Mayor.

In their joy, everyone forgot

the Piper.

Suddenly he appeared
at the Town Hall.
He held out his hand and said:
"Now, please give me
my fifty thousand guilders."
The Mayor's smile disappeared.

"Fifty thousand guilders can buy me
food and wine and jewels,"
the Mayor thought.
"Why should I give so much money
to this man?
After all, the rats are dead.
They cannot come back!"

So the Mayor told the Piper:

"I was only joking

   when I said fifty thousand guilders!

But I will be glad to pay you

   FIFTY guilders. All right?"

At first the Piper was silent.

Then he said,

"Mayor, keep your promise!

If you do not, beware!

You will find that I can pipe

a different tune."

Now the Mayor was angry.

"Are you trying to scare me?"

he said.

"Go on, then! Blow your silly pipe

until you burst!"

The Piper smiled. He left the Mayor

alone in the Town Hall.

The Mayor gave a great sigh of relief.

"Well! That's the end of that!"

he said.

That night, the Mayor was sleeping

when strange music woke him.

He looked out his window.

There in the street

was the Piper, playing a tune.

A soft rustling noise began.

Children came running

from every direction.

Even the Mayor's daughter came.

All the boys and girls of Hamelin

gathered around the Piper

and followed him.

The Mayor and the people of Hamelin

ran out of their houses.

What in the world was happening?

Then they understood.

The Piper was taking their children!

"Stop!" they screamed. "Come back!"

But the children did not listen.

They just kept following the Piper.

He led them to the river,

and then he turned west.

"The Piper is going to the mountain!"

cried the Mayor.

"He will never be able to cross it.

Our children are safe!"

The Piper came to the mountain.

Then an amazing thing happened.

A huge door opened

in the mountainside.

And into the mountain

marched the Piper!

All the children marched in after him.

All but one.

The little lame boy was left behind.

The door in the mountain closed

before he could get inside.

The people of Hamelin wept and wept.

"Bring back our children!"

they cried to the Mayor.

The Mayor sent messengers

east, west, north, and south.

"Tell the Piper I will pay him

anything, anything he wants,"

said the Mayor.

"Only beg him to bring back

our children!"

But it was no use.

The Piper and the children

could not be found.

They were gone forever.

The Mayor had lost

his own little girl

to the Piper. He was so sad,

he could not speak.

At last he gave an order.

"The name of the street

where our children were led away

will be Pied Piper Street.

No music will ever be played

on that street again!"

Then the little lame boy

came hobbling down the street.

"Please, tell us what the Piper said,"

the people asked the boy.

"He said I would go to

a wonderful land, full of flowers

and fruit trees and flying horses.

He said my lame foot would heal

once I got there!"

Two tears rolled down the boy's face.

"But I never did get there," he said.

"And now the door is closed forever."

Hamelin is a real town

in Germany.

Many years ago,

130 children from Hamelin disappeared.

Havel R.

arz Mts.

SAXONY

BOHEMIAN
FOREST

BAVARIA

Where did the children go?

Some think they were stolen

by landowners who needed workers.

Others think the children were taken

to join the famous Children's Crusade.

And some think the children

were really led away

by the Pied Piper.

Nobody knows for sure.

The legend of the Pied Piper

was first made famous

by the Grimm brothers.

It is still told in Hamelin

and all over the world.